MARIA
WENGER

BIRTHDAY
PRESENTS

W9-CHL-953

by Cynthia Rylant

Pictures by

Suçie Stevenson

BIRTHDAY
PRESENTS

A TRUMPET CLUB SPECIAL EDITION

Published by The Trumpet Club
666 Fifth Avenue, New York, New York 10103

Text copyright © 1987 by Cynthia Rylant
Illustrations copyright © 1987 by Suçie Stevenson

All rights reserved. No part of this book may be reproduced or
transmitted in any form or by any means, electronic or mechanical,
including photocopying, recording or by any information storage and
retrieval system, without the written permission of the Publisher, except
where permitted by law. For information address: Orchard Books, a
division of Franklin Watts, Inc., New York, New York.

ISBN 0-440-84679-X

This edition published by arrangement with
Orchard Books, a division of Franklin Watts, Inc.
Book design by Mina Greenstein.

The text of this book is set in 16 pt. Leamington.
The illustrations are watercolor reproduced in full color.

Printed in the United States of America
September 1992

10 9 8 7 6 5 4 3 2 1
DAN

To the Berrigans,
celebrating Sarah and Sam
and my own Nate
— C.R.

W hen you were born
we gave you a kiss. We cried.
We counted all the little piggies
on your hands and feet,
and when we told you we loved you,
you screamed!
Happy birthday.
Your real birthday.

We promised you more . . .

On your first one, we made a star cake,
but since you had only four teeth,
you just sucked the icing off our fingers.

We carried you through the park.
We showed you the trees.
And when we told you we loved you,
you spit up.
Happy birthday.

On your second one,
we made a clown cake.
We invited our friends
but you ignored everybody and wanted only
presents, presents, presents.

You played until you were crabby,
then you cried because you needed a nap.
We laughed.
We told you we loved you.

Then you fell asleep on a quilt on the floor
while we all danced around you in celebration.
Happy birthday.

On your third one, you had the flu,
but we made a train cake anyway.
We chugged it into your room,
and you sat up in bed,
your face all hot and your eyes all big.
You had a caboose and pink medicine.

We took your temperature.
We told you we loved you.
Then we chugged out.
Happy birthday.

On your fourth one, we made a robot cake,
and when you wanted robot plates and cups,
we made those, too.

Three of your friends came
and everyone wanted to play with the toy telephone,
so we had to hide it.

You sat with your friends and everyone giggled
and all of you had chocolate faces,
but you most of all.

And when your friends went home,
we took out the toy telephone
and made calls on it all night.
We dialed your number.
We told you we loved you.
Happy birthday.

On your fifth one,
you wanted the whole kindergarten to come,
but we said no,
our house was too small,
and you understood
and had a party with just us instead.

We made a dinosaur cake,
and you decorated his face,
then we all got stomachaches
from eating a brontosaurus.

You took us through the park,
and you named plants we never knew
and you told us about the moon
and we listened.
We told you we loved you.
Happy birthday.

And before you turned six . . .

Before you turned six,
you gave each of us for our birthdays
flowers that you picked yourself.
You made each of us funny cards
with silly pictures.

DADDY
HAPPY

You helped bake our birthday cakes
and with us you ate too much of them.
You laughed.
You told us you loved us.

And we remembered your real birthday,
when we counted all your little piggies,
when we cried, when you screamed . . .

Birthday presents.